175 Easy-to-Do
CHRISTMAS
CRAFTS

CREATIVE USES · FOR RECYCLABLES ·

Edited by Sharon Dunn Umnik

BOYDS MILLS PRESS

Inside this book...

you'll find a fabulous assortment of crafts made from
recyclable items and inexpensive things found in
or around your house. Have pencils, crayons,
scissors, tape, paintbrushes, and other supplies for
craft making close by. —*the Editor*

Published by Bell Books
Boyds Mills Press, Inc.
A Highlights Company
815 Church Street
Honesdale, Pennsylvania 18431
Printed in the United States of America

Publisher Cataloging-in-Publication Data
175 easy-to-do Christmas crafts : creative uses for recyclables / edited by
Sharon Dunn Umnik.—1st ed.
[64]p. : col. ill. ; cm.
Summary : Includes step-by-step directions to make Christmas ornaments,
decorations, cards, and more. Also includes instructions for making crèches.
ISBN 1-56397-373-1
1. Handicraft—Juvenile literature. 2. Christmas decorations—Juvenile
literature. 3. Recycling (Waste)—Juvenile literature. [1. Handicraft.
2. Christmas decorations. 3. Recycling (Waste).] I. Umnik, Sharon Dunn.
II. Title.
745.5941—dc20   1996   CIP
Library of Congress Catalog Card Number 94-79156

First edition, 1996
Book designed by Charlie Cary
The text of this book is set in 11-point New Century Schoolbook

10 9 8 7 6 5

Craft Contributors: Sharon Addy, Martha Utley Aitken, Karen Wellman Banker, Doris Bartholme,
Katherine Corliss Bartow, Beverly Blasucci, Linda Bloomgren, Betsy Jane Boyd, Doris D. Breiholz,
Dorothy Anderson Burge, Frances M. Callahan, Wilma Cassel, Lydia Cutler, Ronni Davis, Ruth Dougherty,
Donna Dowdy, Kathryn H. Dulan, N.D. Dunlea, Kathy Everett, Susan M. Fisher, Dorothy L. Getchell,
Eugenie Gluckert, Edna Harrington, Mark Haverstock, Zelma Hinkel, Isabel K. Hobba, Carmen Horn,
Rebecca Hubka, Lola J. Janes, Ellen Javernick, Helen Jeffries, Murley K. Kight, Roseanne Kirby, Garnett C.
Kooker, Lillian Koslover, Denise Larson, Jean LaWall, Lee Lindeman, M. Mable Lunz, Agnes Maddy, Paula
Melillo, Dorothy Scott Milke, Blanche B. Mitchell, Joan O'Donnell, Helen M. Pedersen, James W. Perrin Jr.,
Jane K. Priewe, Simone Quick, Roni Reschreiter, Kim Richman, Kathy Ross, Becky Sawyer, Lois Saxelby,
Jane Scherer, Dorothy Snethen, Carle Statter, Jean B. Taylor, Beth Tobler, Sharon Dunn Umnik, Evelyn E.
Uyemura, Deirdre B. Watkins, Agnes Choate Wonson, and Rebecca D. Zurawski.

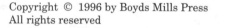

Crèches

"Silent night, holy night ". . . Here are simple Nativities you can make from recycled greeting cards, spice bottles, and a shoe box.

CARD CRÈCHE
(paper towel tube, old greeting cards, heavy cardboard; dried grass, hay, or straw)

1. Using a ruler, mark off 1-inch sections along a paper towel tube. Cut the sections, making 1-inch rings.

2. Cut out figures from old greeting cards. Glue them to the 1-inch tube rings so the figures stand up.

3. Cover a heavy piece of cardboard with glue and dried grass, hay, or straw. Glue the figures in place to form the Nativity scene.

SHOE BOX CRÈCHE
(shoe box and lid, construction paper, poster board, clear plastic wrap)

1. Remove the lid from a shoe box. Glue construction paper to the inside of the box. Cut a 1-inch eyehole in one end of the box.

2. Create Nativity figures from pieces of cut paper. Attach each figure to the box bottom with folded strips of poster board. Keep the figures toward the back half of the box.

3. Cut away one half of the box lid, leaving the rim uncut. Tape clear plastic wrap inside the lid to cover the opening.

4. Cut a small paper star and a strip of poster board. Glue the star to half of the strip. Bend the strip in two and tape the other half to the plastic wrap, above the Nativity figures.

5. Put the lid on the box, and view the scene through the eyehole.

SPICE BOTTLE NATIVITY
(two spice bottles, felt, paper, yarn, cording, jewelry box, cardboard, cotton)

1. To make the heads for Mary and Joseph, trace around a spice-bottle top two times on beige felt and cut out the circles. Glue them to the bottle tops. Cover the sides of the tops with strips of beige felt. Glue on paper eyes and mouths. Add yarn for hair and let dry.

2. To make clothes, glue large strips of felt around the bottles. Cut sleeves and glue at the sides. Place cording for a sash around the waist areas. Add felt hands and feet.

3. For Mary, cut a rectangular shape for the cape, mold it to her body, and glue in place. For Joseph, cut an oval piece of felt and glue it to his head. Add a piece of cording.

4. To make the manger, cover the bottom of a jewelry box with felt. To make the Christ Child, cut a small piece of cardboard. Glue on some cotton. Cover it with felt, making the head and swaddling clothes of Jesus. Add paper eyes and a mouth.

STANDING REINDEER
(bathroom tissue tube, construction paper, yarn, fallen twigs)

1. Cut four sections from one end of a bathroom tissue tube to form the reindeer's four legs.

2. Cut eyes, a nose, and hoofs from construction paper, and glue them in place. Tie a yarn bow around the deer's neck.

3. Using a paper punch, punch a hole on each side of the reindeer's head. Push small twigs through the holes for antlers.

YARN WREATH ORNAMENT
(yarn)

1. Loosely wrap green yarn around your hand about twenty times to form a circle.

2. Cut eight pieces of yarn, each about 6 inches long. Tie each piece, evenly spaced, around the wreath to hold it together. Knot the ends, and trim them with scissors.

3. Decorate the wreath with a red yarn bow. For a hanger, make a loop from a piece of yarn.

EGG-CARTON ANGEL
(cardboard egg carton, poster paint, 1 1/2-inch plastic-foam ball, yarn, paper)

1. Cut out a small, a medium, and a large pillar section from a cardboard egg carton, as shown.

2. Glue all three sections together for the body, with the largest on the bottom and the smallest on the top.

3. Cut wings from the lid, and glue them to the body. Cover the body with white poster paint and let dry.

4. For the head, glue a 1 1/2-inch plastic-foam ball. Glue on yarn hair and features cut from paper.

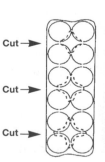

Cut →
Cut →
Cut →

PINECONE PLACE CARDS
(pinecones, green paper, glitter, ribbon)

1. Collect one pinecone for each family member. Rinse the pinecones with water, and let them dry on a paper towel.

2. Cut a holly-leaf shape from green paper for each pinecone.

3. Print each person's name on a leaf. Squeeze white glue around the edge, and sprinkle it with glitter.

4. Glue each holly leaf into a pinecone. Add a ribbon bow at the top.

JINGLE-BELL SHAKER
(large thread spool, construction paper, felt, pencil, bells, yarn, white tape)

1. Trace around the top of a large thread spool two times on construction paper. Cut out the circles and glue one on each end of the spool. Let dry.

2. Cut holly leaves and berries from pieces of felt. Glue them on the sides of the spool.

3. Poke a pencil through the paper at each spool hole. String three bells on a 12-inch piece of yarn. Put the two ends of the yarn through the holes in the spool.

4. Hold the yarn ends with one hand and push a pencil into the bottom of the spool for a handle. Tie the yarn ends around the pencil, forming a bow. Wrap the pencil completely with white tape.

SANTA MAILBAG
(construction paper, 6-by-12-inch brown paper bag, cotton balls, self-adhesive reinforcement rings, ribbon)

1. Cut and glue red construction paper to cover the lower three-fourths of a 6-by-12-inch brown paper bag.

2. Cut a 4-inch circle of paper for the face, a red triangle for the hat, and a small white circle and strip for the trim on the hat. Glue in place. Glue cotton balls on the trim of the hat.

3. Add eyes, a nose, and a mouth from paper. Glue on cotton balls for eyebrows, a mustache, and a beard. Glue paper mittens, buttons, a belt, and boots in place.

4. On the back of the bag near the top, place two self-adhesive reinforcement rings about 2 inches apart. Make a hole through the centers, and string a ribbon through for hanging.

CHRISTMAS TREE CARD
(plastic-foam tray, poster board, construction paper)

1. Wash and dry a small plastic-foam tray. Draw a picture of a tree on the tray, and cut it out.

2. Glue the tree to the front of a folded piece of poster board.

3. Glue paper-punch dots to the tree.

CLOTHESPIN BIRD ORNAMENT
(paper, paint, spring-type clothespin)

1. Place two sheets of paper one on top of the other. Draw the side view of a bird on the top piece. Holding both sheets, cut around the bird. Decorate the edges with a marker.

2. Paint a spring-type clothespin to match the color of your paper and let it dry.

3. Glue the birds across from each other, one on each side of the clothespin. Let dry.

4. Clip the bird onto a branch of your Christmas tree.

SANTA DECORATION
(wire clothes hanger, construction paper, three plastic bottle caps, string)

1. Pull down the bottom of a wire clothes hanger until the hanger is diamond-shaped.

2. To form Santa's hat, cut two pieces of red construction paper into triangles slightly wider than the top half of the hanger. Glue the edges of the triangles together, leaving an opening at the very top and bottom. Slip the hat over the hanger, with the hook poking through the opening at the peak. Glue on white pieces of paper to decorate the hat.

3. Fold an 18-by-8-inch piece of white paper in half for the beard. Cut slits through both thicknesses to about 2 inches from the fold. Roll the strips around a pencil to curl them. Hang the paper over the bottom of the hanger, and attach it with glue.

4. For the eyes and nose, tie and glue a long string around each plastic bottle cap and tape each string to the inside of the hat. Make a mustache from white paper, and glue it to the beard. Use a marker to draw on a mouth.

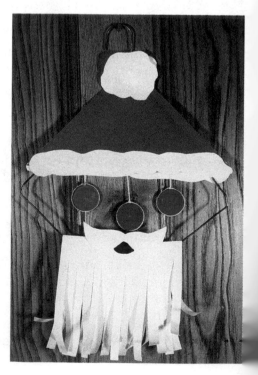

DOORKNOB WREATH
(felt, cardboard, glitter, sequins)

1. Cut out a 4-inch circle from a piece of red felt and a thin piece of cardboard. Glue them together.

2. Make a dot in the center of the cardboard. Draw an X through the dot. Cut along the lines of the X.

3. Cut several holly leaves from green felt, and cut berries from red felt. Glue the leaves around the outside edge of the circle, then add the berries. Glue on sequins and glitter.

4. Slip the wreath over a doorknob.

JIGSAW PUZZLE
(old greeting card, poster board, envelope)

1. Choose an old greeting card that has a festive holiday scene on it. Cut a piece of poster board the same size as the greeting card.

2. Spread a thin layer of glue on the poster board and glue the greeting card to it. Let dry.

3. On the back of the poster board, draw a pattern for the puzzle pieces, dividing the board into about twelve pieces. Carefully cut along the lines of the pattern.

4. Put the puzzle pieces in an envelope and give to a friend.

GLITTER-STAR ORNAMENT
(waxed paper, white glue, glitter)

1. Place a piece of waxed paper on your work surface.

2. Draw a star shape on the waxed paper using white glue. Add a loop at one point.

3. Sprinkle glitter onto the glue. Let dry.

4. Gently peel the paper away from the star. Hang the star by the loop on your holiday tree, or attach a ribbon to the loop and hang the star in your window.

SLEIGH CARDHOLDER
(cereal box, paint, poster board)

1. Cut a section from a cereal box to make the holder. Cover the cutout section with red paint and let it dry.

2. Draw runners for the sleigh on black poster board. Cut out the runners and glue them in place.

3. Fill the sleigh with holiday cards.

EVERGREEN BALL
(apple, ribbon, wooden skewer, evergreens)

1. Tie a ribbon around a firm apple, the way you would tie a package, so that the apple can be hung.

2. Collect several different kinds of evergreens. Poke holes in the apple using a small wooden skewer. Push a piece of greenery firmly into each hole.

3. Continue until the apple is covered. The juice from the apple will keep the evergreens fresh. Hang the evergreen ball in a window or a doorway.

PAPER-PLATE ANGEL
(paper plate, quarter, glitter, string)

1. Divide a paper plate into four parts, as shown. On the center line, below the rim, trace around a quarter to make the head. Draw the body and arms, as shown.

2. Cut the plate apart along the dotted lines. The shaded areas are left over but will be used later.

3. Tape the narrow ends of the arms behind the body, with the backs of the plate facing outward. Glue the wing sections the same way, with half of each wing visible.

4. To make the halo, cut a curved piece from one of the leftover pieces and glue it to the top of the head. Add hands and feet.

5. Spread glue and add glitter. Glue a loop of string to the back of the head.

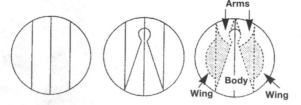

FILM CANISTER ORNAMENT
(old greeting cards, 35mm plastic film canister, ribbon, rickrack)

1. Cut out holiday pictures from old greeting cards. Trim them to the size of a 35mm plastic film canister.

2. Glue the pictures to the outside of the canister.

3. To make the hanger, glue a piece of ribbon underneath the lid. When it is dry, replace the lid on the canister.

4. Decorate the canister with rickrack.

TREE SKIRT
(fabric)

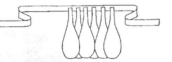

1. Draw and cut out a teardrop-shaped pattern on an 18-by-7-inch piece of paper.

2. Place the pattern on a piece of fabric 2 yards wide and 20 inches long. Pin to hold. *Ask an adult to help you* cut around the pattern, using sewing scissors or a pair of pinking shears for a saw-toothed edge. Cut ten to twelve teardrop shapes.

3. Cut a strip of fabric about 3 1/2 inches wide and 2 yards long. Staple the narrow end of one teardrop shape to the center of the strip of cloth. Continue to staple the teardrops on either side of the center, overlapping each teardrop halfway.

4. Place the skirt around the base of your tree, and tie the ends of the strip into a bow.

CANDLE HOLDER
(two baby-food jars, sand, twine, felt, glitter, candle, salt)

1. Wash and dry two baby-food jars. Fill one jar with sand and attach the lid.

2. Spread glue, starting at the edge of the lid. Place an end of twine in the glue and wrap the twine around the jar. Add more glue and continue until the jar is completely covered. (Do not cover the top or the bottom of the jar.) Cover the other jar, without a lid, in the same way.

3. Glue the two jars together, keeping the one filled with sand on the bottom. Decorate with a poinsettia flower made from felt. Add glitter.

4. Place a candle in the jar, and pour salt around it to hold it in place.

PAPER-PLATE CHRISTMAS TREE
(two 9-inch paper plates, watercolors, poster board, self-adhesive reinforcement rings, glitter, yarn)

1. Paint two 9-inch white paper plates with green watercolor. Cut both plates in half, then cut one section in half again.

2. On a square piece of red poster board, arrange the plate pieces to form a tree shape, and glue in place. Attach a brown-paper tree trunk.

3. Color self-adhesive reinforcement rings with markers. Place the rings on the tree. Drop glue inside each hole, and sprinkle it with glitter.

4. Add a glittery star to the top of the tree. Then glue a piece of yarn to the back for a hanger.

FRAMED ORNAMENT
(frozen-juice pull-top lid, old greeting card, ribbon)

1. Wash a frozen-juice pull-top lid and let dry.

2. Place the lid on a design of an old greeting card, and trace around it. Cut a little inside the traced line. Glue the design inside the rim of the lid.

3. Glue a thin piece of ribbon to the back of the ornament for a hanger.

PRINCE OF THE KINGDOM OF SWEETS
(46-ounce beverage can, construction paper, cardboard, poster paint, 2-liter beverage bottle, yarn, old newspaper)

1. Use a 46-ounce beverage can for the prince's body. Glue on pieces of construction paper to decorate.

2. For the feet, trace around the bottom of the can on a piece of cardboard. Draw feet that stick out from the circle and cut them out. Paint the feet black and, when they are dry, glue them to the can.

3. For the hat, remove the black plastic bottom from a 2-liter beverage bottle. To make a strap, tape the ends of a piece of yarn to the inside. Crumple up some old newspaper and stuff it into the hat so it doesn't fall down over the prince's eyes.

4. Place the hat on top of the prince and adjust the yarn so it goes across where his mouth would be.

SANTA DOOR DECORATION
(corrugated cardboard, fabric, white plastic table cover, acrylic paint,
1 1/2-inch plastic-foam ball, string)

1. For Santa's body, cut a large triangle from corrugated cardboard. Starting at the point of the triangle, staple or tape red fabric for the hat, beige fabric for the head, and red fabric for the body.

2. Cut a cardboard strip and cover it with white plastic for the brim of the hat. Staple it to the hat.

3. Cut a cardboard beard shape and cover it with white plastic. Cut strips of plastic, loop them, and staple them to the beard.

4. Add paper eyes and eyebrows. For the nose, paint a 1 1/2-inch plastic-foam ball and glue it in place. Cut boots from cardboard and cover with black fabric.

5. Glue a loop of string to the back. Hang your Santa where he won't get wet.

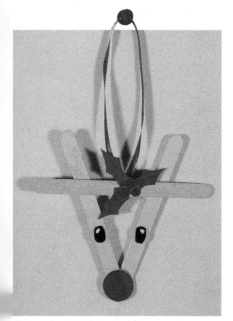

● ●

A REINDEER
(three ice-cream sticks, construction paper, ribbon)

1. Glue three ice-cream sticks together in an A shape and let dry.

2. Turn the A shape upside down. Decorate with a paper nose, eyes, holly leaves, and berries.

3. Add a piece of ribbon to the back with glue, and hang the reindeer on your holiday tree.

NOTE PAD
(old greeting card, cardboard, paper)

1. Cut around a picture from an old greeting card to make the front of the note pad.

2. Place the picture on a piece of cardboard and trace around it. Cut out the cardboard to use as the back of the note pad.

3. Stack some sheets of white paper. Place the picture on the top sheet of paper and trace around the picture. Holding the sheets of paper together, cut out the shape.

4. Place the sheets of paper between the picture and the cardboard back. Staple together at the top.

EGG-CARTON CAROLERS
(gift wrap, plastic-foam egg carton, construction paper, yarn)

1. Glue gift wrap to the top of a plastic-foam egg carton, tucking the edges inside the carton. Turn the carton over.

2. With a paper punch, punch pieces of construction paper for eyes and mouths, and glue them to the twelve egg sections. Cut bow ties from paper and glue them in place.

3. For the hair, glue strands of yarn to the top of each head. Draw on noses.

4. Write the name of your favorite Christmas carol on a strip of paper and glue it to the front.

SANTA SNOWBALL TOSS
(cardboard box, construction paper, three 2-inch plastic-foam balls)

1. Cover the bottom and sides of a rectangular cardboard box with construction paper.

2. On a piece of paper, draw a Santa face with a large mouth. Paint or color the face with markers. Glue it to the box and cut out the large mouth.

To play: Place Santa against a wall. Give each player three tries at throwing 2-inch plastic-foam balls into Santa's mouth. See who can get all three into Santa.

THREE-IN-ONE BELL
(construction paper, string)

1. Glue two contrasting colors of construction paper together. Fold the paper in half, and cut a large bell (number 1) on the fold.

2. Starting at the lower part of the bell, cut two additional bells (number 2 and 3), leaving 1/2 inch at the top of the bells uncut.

3. Open the bells. On the right side of the bell cut directly to the fold. On the left side cut diagonally to the fold. Turn the bells to go in different directions.

4. Attach a string to the bell and hang the decoration.

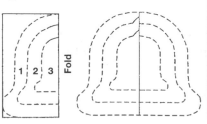

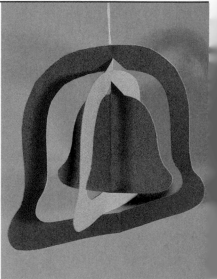

REINFORCEMENT RING CARD
(construction paper, self-adhesive reinforcement rings)

1. Fold a piece of construction paper in half, forming a card. On the front of the card, place self-adhesive reinforcement rings in a holiday shape.

2. Add a colorful bow for decoration. Write a message inside.

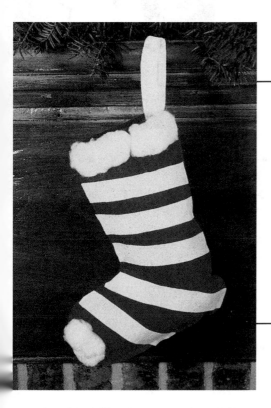

CHRISTMAS STOCKING
(lightweight cardboard, felt, cotton)

1. Draw a stocking pattern on a piece of cardboard and cut it out. Trace around the pattern on two pieces of felt. Cut out the stockings.

2. Spread glue around the edges of one stocking. Place the other stocking on top and let it dry.

3. Decorate the front with other pieces of felt and cotton. Staple a loop of felt to the stocking to make a hanger.

ICICLE ORNAMENTS
(clear plastic lids, white tissue paper, water, white glue, cup, ribbon)

1. Cut icicle shapes from large clear plastic lids. Cut or tear white tissue paper into small pieces.

2. Mix even amounts of water and white glue in a small cup. Brush a small amount of the glue solution on the icicle and press pieces of tissue paper into the glue, giving the icicle texture. Repeat until you have covered the entire icicle, back and front. Let dry.

3. Punch a small hole at the top of each icicle and tie a loop of ribbon.

SNOWMAN CARD
(white paper)

1. Cut a piece of white paper 10 by 8 inches. Fold it in half to measure 5 by 4 inches.

2. Draw a snowman starting with the top of his hat at the fold line, and work down to the bottom of the paper.

3. Cut along the drawing of the snowman, but do not cut along the fold at the top of his hat.

4. Decorate the snowman with markers and write a message inside.

PLASTIC-FOAM ORNAMENT
(cookie cutter, plastic-foam tray, ball-point pen cap, ribbon)

1. Press a holiday cookie cutter on a flat, clean, white plastic-foam tray. Cut out the shape following the pressed line.

2. Use the open end of a ball-point pen cap and press circles into the ornament, making a design. Poke out the center of each circle with a pencil.

3. Punch a hole at the top of the ornament, and tie a ribbon for a hanger.

WALNUT-SHELL CRADLE
(walnut-shell half, cotton, fabric, button, paper)

1. Use a walnut-shell half for the cradle. Stuff a bit of cotton into the shell. Lay a small piece of white fabric over the cotton to serve as a bottom sheet. Tuck the edges in and add glue to hold in place.

2. Glue a piece of paper on top of a button. Draw on facial features with a marker. Glue the button face partly on the sheet and partly on the walnut-shell edge.

3. Cut a piece of white fabric for the top sheet and a piece of colored fabric for the blanket. Tuck the edges in and add glue.

4. Make a hanger by adding a loop of yarn to the cradle bottom.

FABRIC WREATH
(wire clothes hanger, fabric)

1. Bend and shape the triangular section of a wire clothes hanger into a circle.

2. Cut fabric into strips about 5 inches long and a 1/2 inch wide.

3. Tie the strips to the hanger. The more strips you use, the fuller the wreath will become.

4. Add a bow cut from fabric.

CHRISTMAS FRAME
(four tongue depressors, acrylic paint, poster board, ribbon, string, photo)

1. Glue four tongue depressors together to form a square frame.

2. Paint the frame with a couple of coats of acrylic paint, letting each coat dry before adding another.

3. Cut four small squares from poster board. Decorate them with ribbon to look like packages. Glue one package to each corner.

4. Glue a string hanger to the back and let dry. Cut a photo to fit the frame and tape it on the back.

SANTA CLAUS MASK
(large paper bag, construction paper)

1. Measure about 4 inches from the opening of a large paper bag, and cut around the entire bag. Glue a piece of construction paper on the front side of the bag.

2. Put the bag on your head. Using a crayon, have a friend carefully mark where the eyeholes should be. Remove the bag. Cut out the eyeholes.

3. To make a hat, glue a large piece of red paper from the front to the back of the bag. Add facial features from paper and glue in place. Add a white paper beard. Cut slits into the bottom and sides of the paper. Curl the edges of the beard by rolling them around a pencil.

4. Add small strips of paper to trim the hat. Wear a red sweat shirt when you put on the mask.

HAND AND FOOT ANGEL
(poster board, cardboard, chenille stick, paper, ribbon, glitter, large paper clip)

1. To make the angel body, place your foot on white poster board with cardboard underneath the poster board. Trace around your foot with a pencil, and cut out the shape.

2. To make the wings, trace around your hands on yellow poster board. Cut out the shapes, and glue one to each side of the body.

3. To make the halo, form a circle with a chenille stick. Glue it to the back of the angel. Create a face with markers and paper cutouts. Use ribbon for hair. Spread glue on the wings, and sprinkle them with glitter.

4. Bend open a large paper clip, and tape it to the back as a hanger.

SILVER DOOR BOW
(three 8-inch aluminum pie tins, chenille stick, ribbon, string)

1. Cut off and discard the heavy outer rim of three 8-inch aluminum pie tins. Cut each tin into one long, continuous strip, about 1/4 inch wide, starting at the outer edge, continuing around, and ending at the tin's center.

2. To create the bow, make a loop for one side of the bow, then another loop for the other side, holding the strip firmly at the center. Continue making these loops from one side to the other, reaching the curl that was the center of the tin. Let this end hang down for the bow end. Twist a chenille stick around the center to hold.

3. Following step 2, create a bow with each of the other two strips of foil. Fasten all three bows together to form one large bow with a chenille stick in the center.

4. Add green and red ribbon to the foil. Add a string loop to hang.

HOLLY CHAIN
(green and red construction paper)

1. Fold a 3-by-4-inch piece of green construction paper in half, the long way. Draw half of a double holly leaf and cut it out along the dotted lines, as shown.

2. Fold back the center of the leaf at the solid line. Cut several leaves. Hook each leaf underneath the next one to make a chain.

3. Cut and glue red berries along the holly.

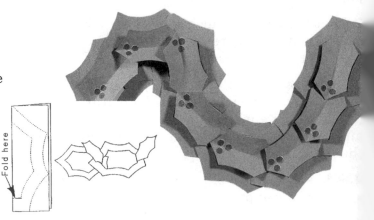

Fold here

THREE-DIMENSIONAL CARD
(small gift box, paper, green poster board)

1. Use a small white gift box, or cover a small box with white paper. Draw and cut out a tree shape from the center of the lid. Discard the cutout tree and keep the lid.

2. Glue green paper inside the box. Glue red strips of paper on the green paper. Glue the lid on the box. Add paper cutouts.

3. Write a greeting on the lid with a marker. Glue the box to a piece of green poster board that is larger than the box.

YARN SNOWFLAKES
(old newspaper, disposable container, yarn, large plastic lid, glitter, heavy thread)

1. Cover your work space with old newspaper. Squeeze white glue into a disposable container. Dip pieces of yarn in the glue. Press the pieces of yarn through your fingers to remove excess glue.

2. Place pieces of the glue-covered yarn on a large plastic lid, creating snowflake shapes. Let dry.

3. Peel the shapes away from the lid. Brush a little glue on each snowflake and sprinkle them with glitter. Let dry.

4. Add a thread-loop hanger.

CHRISTMAS CORSAGE
(poster board, ribbon, two 1-inch plastic-foam balls, table knife, yarn, sequins, moveable plastic eyes, chenille stick)

1. Cut a large bow shape from a piece of poster board for the base of the corsage. Add pieces of cut ribbon.

2. Cut two 1-inch plastic-foam balls in half with a table knife. Glue three halves on top of the ribbon. (Save the leftover one for another project.)

3. Glue pieces of yellow yarn for hair. Add sequin mouths and moveable plastic eyes.

4. To make halos, cut three pieces from a chenille stick and glue them in place.

NAPKIN RING
(red and green felt)

1. For the ring, cut a rectangular shape about 3 inches wide and 6 inches long from red felt.

2. For the leaf, cut a 4-inch square from green felt. For the flower, cut two 3-inch squares from red felt.

3. Trim the shapes, as shown. Cut a slit in the middle of the leaf and flowers.

4. Slip the ends of the ring shape first through the leaf and then through the two flowers.

Ring Leaf Flower

3" 6" 4" 4" Cut a slit 3" 3" 3"

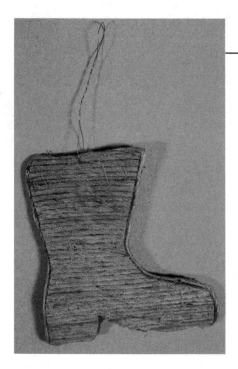

TWINE ORNAMENT
(heavy cardboard, twine, sewing needle, thread)

1. Cut out an ornament shape from heavy cardboard.

2. Cover one side with glue. Press pieces of twine into the glue and let dry. Trim away the excess twine when dry. Glue twine to the other side of the ornament in the same way.

3. To outline the ornament, soak twine in warm water so it will be easy to work with. Remove the twine from the water and dry it off with a cloth.

4. Spread glue around the edge of the shape and press the twine into it. Use a needle and thread to make a loop hanger.

MRS. CLAUS PUPPET
(small soup box, construction paper, cotton balls, paper doily, small ornaments)

1. Secure the top of a small soup box with tape, and cover the box with construction paper.

2. Cut through the box at the center, leaving the back uncut. Cut and glue paper features for the face, using the cut at the center as the mouth. Add cotton for eyebrows and hair. Glue on a paper collar and a piece of doily for trim.

3. Make a hat from paper and add cotton for the trim. Glue the hat in place. Add small ornaments as earrings.

4. Cut two small holes through the back, one at the top for your index finger and one at the bottom for your thumb to fit into. Work the puppet with your fingers inside the holes.

RING WREATH
(cardboard, paper towel tubes, poster paint, beads, paper, tissue, string)

1. To make the base for the wreath, *ask an adult to help you* cut a 7-inch-wide circle from cardboard. Measure 2 inches from the outer edge and draw a smaller circle inside. Cut out a 3-inch circle from the center.

2. Cut off ten 1-inch rings from cardboard tubes. Cut a zigzag or scalloped edge on one side of each ring. Glue the flat side of the rings onto the base of the wreath and let dry.

3. Paint the rings and the base green and let them dry. Add another coat of paint.

4. Add beads and cut-paper holly leaves to the edge of the wreath. Wad up some tissue and glue it in one of the rings, filling it. Glue a paper bow on top of the tissue. Add a loop of string to the back for a hanger.

BELL COOKIE-CUTTER ORNAMENT
(string, bell, metal cookie cutter, ribbon)

1. Tie one end of a piece of string to a small bell. Tie the other end of it to a bell-shaped cookie cutter so the small bell hangs in the center of the cookie cutter.

2. Cover the outside of the cookie cutter with ribbon, making a loop at the top for a hanger. Let dry.

REINDEER CUTOUTS
(paper)

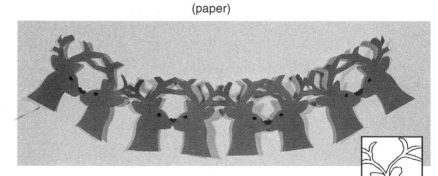

1. Cut a strip of paper about 16 inches long and 3 1/2 inches wide. Fold it in half three times.

2. With the folds at the sides, draw a reindeer's head. Bring the tip of the nose and two antlers to the edge of the right side, and two antlers to the edge of the left side, as shown in the diagram.

3. Keeping the paper folded, cut out the reindeer. Do not cut on the fold. Open the chain. Color the noses and draw eyes.

RECYCLED CARD
(white paper, ribbon, old greeting card)

1. Fold a sheet of 8 1/2-by-11-inch paper in half twice, forming a card.

2. Cut pieces of ribbon and glue around the edges of the front of the card.

3. Cut out a design from an old greeting card and glue it in the middle of the ribbon border.

4. Write a message inside.

QUILTED ORNAMENT
(fabric, 3-inch plastic-foam ball, table knife, straight pin, ribbon)

1. Cut small pieces of fabric in different shapes. Place one piece on a 3-inch plastic-foam ball. Gently press the corners of the fabric into the ball with a table knife.

2. To place the second piece of fabric, overlap one edge of the first piece of fabric, and press in. Continue until the entire ball is covered.

3. Fold a piece of ribbon so the ends overlap. Stick a straight pin through the overlap, and pin the ribbon to the quilted ball so the ornament can be hung.

SANTA CANDY HOLDER
(poster board, white paper, cardboard egg carton)

1. Cut a large half circle, about 12 inches across, from red poster board. Cut a smaller half circle, about 6 inches across. Form each into a cone and staple the ends.

2. Cut a piece of white paper for the face. Fringe and curl the edges of the paper to make a beard, and add eyes and a nose. Glue the face to the larger cone.

3. To make a tassel, poke some thin white strips of paper through the top of the small cone, and glue them in place. Glue the small cone on top of the larger one.

4. Cut cups from a cardboard egg carton and glue around the bottom of the Santa. Fill the cups with treats.

THE CHRISTMAS MOUSE
(construction paper, yarn)

1. Cut three large circles from gray paper and three smaller circles from pink paper. Glue a pink circle in the middle of each gray circle.

2. Glue the three circles together to form the head and ears of the mouse. Draw facial features with a marker.

3. Cut two small holly leaves from green paper and berries from red paper. Glue them to the mouse's head.

4. Glue a loop of yarn behind the head for a hanger.

HOLIDAY SWEAT SHIRT
(cardboard, white sweat shirt, green fabric paint, sewing needle, embroidery floss, buttons)

1. Draw and cut out a tree shape from the center of a piece of cardboard, making a stencil.

2. Lay the sweat shirt flat on your work surface. Place another piece of cardboard inside the sweat shirt. Tape the stencil on the front of the sweat shirt. Paint the inside of the stencil with green fabric paint. Follow the directions on the paint bottle for drying time.

3. With a needle and embroidery floss, sew different-colored buttons of different sizes all over the tree as ornaments.

COTTON-BALL SNOWMAN
(poster board, felt, cotton balls, fabric, yarn)

1. From poster board, cut the shape of a snowman wearing a hat. Cover the hat with glue and a piece of felt. Trim around the edges with scissors. Add felt decorations.

2. Glue cotton balls over the body of the snowman. Glue pieces of felt for the face and buttons. Tie a strip of fabric around the neck for a scarf.

3. Use a small piece of yarn for a hanger, and glue it to the back of the snowman's hat.

YARN CHRISTMAS BELLS
(different-sized plastic cups, yarn, bells)

1. Cover the outside of three cups with glue, and wind yarn around each cup. Poke a small hole in the bottom of each cup with a pencil.

2. Cut three long pieces of yarn. Attach a bell to the end of each piece. Make a knot about 1 to 2 inches above each bell.

3. Thread the loose ends of yarn through the cup holes. Tie the cups together at different lengths.

TUBE ORNAMENT
(bathroom tissue tube, poster paint, glitter, lace, ribbon)

1. Cut the ends of a bathroom tissue tube into fringes, scallops, or points. Cover the tube with poster paint and let dry.

2. Decorate with glue, glitter, and lace. Punch a hole on opposite sides of the tube and tie a piece of ribbon for hanging.

FELT HANDPRINT
(felt, poster board, old newspaper, tempera paint, paper plate, cording, sequins)

1. Cut a piece of felt about 8 by 11 inches. Glue it to a piece of poster board and trim around the edges with scissors.

2. Cover your work area with old newspaper. Pour a small amount of white tempera paint onto a large paper plate. Place your hand in the paint until your palm and all of your fingers are covered. Let the excess paint drip off your hand.

3. Carefully place your hand on the felt. (Do not wiggle your hand or you will smear the print.) Then slowly lift your hand, holding the felt down with your clean hand. Let dry.

4. Punch a hole in each top corner and tie a piece of cording from one hole to the other for a hanger.

5. Using a marker, print "Merry Christmas" across the top of the handprint. Sign your name at the bottom. Decorate with sequins. (Add the date if you wish.)

SANTA NAPKIN HOLDER
(felt, red napkin)

1. To make each napkin holder, cut a beard shape from white felt, as shown. Fold a red napkin.

2. Place the felt piece on top of the napkin. Fold the ends behind the napkin and glue or staple them together.

3. Add eyes and a mouth from felt and glue in place.

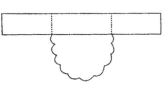

CANDY-CANE REINDEER
(candy cane, moveable plastic eyes, pompon, chenille stick, felt, string)

1. Hold a candy cane so that its curved top faces you. This part will be the reindeer's face. Keeping the wrapper on the candy cane, glue moveable plastic eyes and a red pompon to the reindeer's face.

2. Twist a brown chenille stick around the top of the head, and bend to create antlers. Add smaller pieces of chenille stick to make points on the antlers.

3. Cut a piece of felt in the shape of a bow tie. Glue onto the neck.

4. Tie a loop of string behind the antlers, and display the reindeer on your tree.

CANDLE CARD
(white poster board, paper, felt)

1. Fold a piece of white poster board to form a card. Cut and glue a piece of paper on the front of the card.

2. Cut 1-inch-square pieces of felt. Cut these into smaller pieces and glue them to the front of the card, creating a candle shape.

3. Add a paper base and flame to the candle. Write a greeting inside the card.

CHRISTMAS CARD HOLDER
(cardboard, burlap, felt, paper, cotton, spring-type clothespin, yarn)

1. Cut a 10-inch-square piece of cardboard. Cut a piece of burlap about a 1/2-inch larger than the cardboard. Glue it on top of the cardboard. Pull a few strands of the burlap to fringe the edges.

2. To make Santa, cut a cardboard triangle. Cut and glue black-felt boots to the bottom of the triangle. Glue red felt on top of the triangle. Add paper eyes and cotton hair, beard, and trim for the hat.

3. Glue one side of a spring-type clothespin in the center of the burlap square. (Keep the closed end facing downward.) Glue the Santa on the other side of the clothespin with the boots at the closed end of the clothespin.

4. Glue a piece of yarn to the back for a hanger.

"GINGERBREAD-BOY" ORNAMENT
(corrugated cardboard, paper, yarn)

1. Draw a gingerbread boy shape on a piece of corrugated cardboard. Cut out.

2. Glue pink yarn around the edges to look as if he is trimmed with frosting.

3. Punch circles of colored paper to make buttons, cheeks, and eyes. Glue them in place.

4. Punch a hole in the top of the boy, and tie a piece of yarn for a hanger.

NOEL PLAQUE
(heavy cardboard, fabric, decorative trim, old greeting card, glitter)

1. Cut a rectangular shape from heavy cardboard. Glue fabric on the front and wrap the excess on the back. Attach decorative trim at the top and bottom edges.

2. Select the front of an old greeting card and glue to the fabric. Write the word "Noel" on the fabric with white glue and carefully sprinkle glitter. Let dry.

3. Glue a piece of decorative trim on the back as a hanger.

STRING AND TISSUE FUN
(waxed paper, white glue, disposable container, water, tissue paper, white string)

1. Cover your work space with waxed paper. Squeeze white glue in a disposable container and stir in a little water. Place a piece of colored tissue paper on top of the waxed paper.

2. Dip pieces of white string in the glue. Pull the pieces of string through your fingers to remove excess glue.

3. Place the glue-soaked strings on the tissue paper, making a shape. Carefully place another piece of tissue paper on top of the shape. Press down gently along the string. Let dry.

4. Trim the tissue paper close to the dried string.

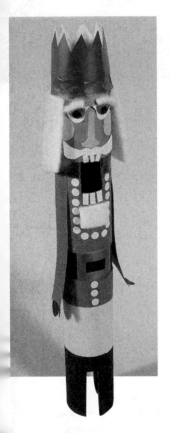

THE NUTCRACKER
(paper, 12-inch paper towel tube, fuzzy fabric)

1. To make boots, cut a strip of black paper 2 1/2 by 6 inches. Start at one end of a 12-inch paper towel tube and glue the paper around the tube. Cut a small section from the center.

2. Cut a strip of yellow paper 2 by 6 inches. Glue it above the boots to make pants. Cut a strip of red paper 1 by 6 inches. Glue it above the pants to make the bottom of the jacket.

3. Cut a strip of black paper 1 by 6 inches. Glue it above the jacket bottom for a belt. Cut a strip of red paper 2 1/2 by 6 inches for the top of the jacket.

4. Cut a strip of gold paper 1/4 by 6 inches. Glue it above the jacket for the collar. Cut and glue a strip of brown paper to cover the rest of the tube. Cut a strip of paper with saw-toothed edges and glue at the top for a crown.

5. Cut a hole for the mouth. Cut and glue strips of paper for arms. Add black gloves and gold paper trim. Add facial features from cut paper. Use pieces of fuzzy fabric for hair, eyebrows, and a beard.

PACKAGE PIN
(cardboard, fabric, ribbon, safety pin)

1. Cover a small square of cardboard with fabric. Glue a ribbon around it to look like a package.

2. Glue a safety pin to the back and wear it on a shirt or sweater.

ANGEL
(paper plate, chenille stick, aluminum foil, ribbon, thread)

1. To make the angel's shape, cut a paper plate, as shown. Fold the plate back to make the angel's body. Fold the plate forward to make the angel's wings.

2. To make the angel's hair, wrap a chenille stick around a pencil. Slide the curled stick off the pencil, and glue it around the angel's face. Add features to the face with markers.

3. For the gown, glue on a piece of aluminum foil. Add a bow made from ribbon.

4. Tie a piece of thread through the top of the hair for a hanger.

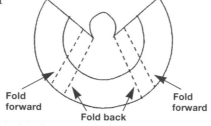

Fold forward

Fold back

Fold forward

PATCHWORK ORNAMENTS
(plastic-foam trays, scrap fabric, thread)

1. Cut ornament shapes from plastic-foam trays.

2. Glue patches of scrap fabric onto the ornaments until they are completely covered.

3. Poke a hole at the top of each ornament and attach a thread-loop hanger.

HOLIDAY POSTCARDS
(old greeting cards)

1. Use the picture panels of old greeting cards to create holiday postcards. Cut the picture panel from the verse panel. (The postal minimum size is 3 1/2 by 5 inches, the maximum size is 4 1/4 by 6 inches.)

2. On the back of the picture panel, draw a line to create message and address sections.

3. Attach a stamp in the upper right-hand corner of the postcard.

NAPKIN HOLDER
(plastic detergent bottle, felt, lace, sequins)

1. On each side of a clear plastic detergent bottle, draw the shape shown, starting an inch up from the bottom. Cut along the line and discard the top and side parts.

2. Cut and glue a piece of felt to cover the front and back of the holder. Glue a lace ruffle around the bottom.

3. Cut and glue a felt tree to each side of the holder. Decorate with sequins and let dry.

SANTA TISSUE BOX
(red tissue paper, unopened box of facial tissues, cotton ball, white paper)

1. Use a double-folded sheet of red tissue paper that is long enough to cover an unopened box of facial tissues and to extend beyond it for the hat, as shown. Cover three sides. Cover the fourth side only up to the slot through which the facial tissues will be removed. This will be the back.

2. Gather the hat into a point and staple. Glue on a cotton ball.

3. For the face and beard, cut three pieces of white paper to cover the front and to overlap 1 1/2 inches on each side. Scallop the bottoms with scissors and glue the pieces on separately. Add eyes and a mouth from paper.

4. Glue a white-paper band around the base of the hat and coat. Trim at the bottom of the box. Add a black belt and white buckle.

GIFT WRAP PHOTO FRAME
(lightweight cardboard, gift wrap)

1. Cut two rectangular pieces of lightweight cardboard the same size, one for the back section and one for the front section. Cut out from the front section an area large enough to fit a photo.

2. Cover the pieces of cardboard with gift wrap and tape down. To cut out the section for the photo, cut an X from corner to corner and fold back the paper, trim, and glue.

3. Place a photo in the opening, and tape it to the back of the front section. Glue the two cardboard sections together.

4. Cut a small piece of cardboard, and cover it with paper. Glue it in the middle of the back of the frame so it stands up.

ANGEL MOBILE
(poster board, string, plastic-foam trays, bells)

1. Cut a large star shape from a piece of yellow poster board. Holding the star with two points up, punch a hole between the two points and tie a long string for a hanger.

2. Draw an angel pattern on paper and cut it out. Trace and cut out three angels from plastic-foam trays. Punch a hole at the top and bottom of each one.

3. Punch a hole at the tip of three points of the star. With string, tie one angel to each point of the star.

4. Tie a bell to the bottom of each angel. Hang the mobile in a window or doorway.

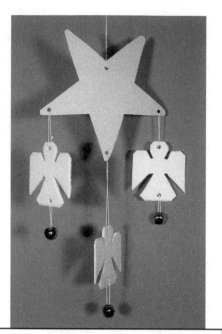

STAND-UP GREETING
(poster board)

1. Fold a long piece of poster board in half. Open the card, and draw a stocking on the front. Write the name of a family member or friend at the top of the stocking.

2. Cut around the stocking outline just to the fold of the poster board. Fold the card so the stocking will stand up.

3. Write a greeting inside.

LACY TREE ORNAMENT
(waxed paper, four ice-cream sticks, paint, paper doily, string)

1. Place waxed paper on your work surface. Paint four ice-cream sticks. Let dry between two coats of paint.

2. Glue the sticks together in the centers, one on top of the other. Place a piece of waxed paper and a heavy object on top of the sticks to press them together.

3. After they have dried, decorate with pieces cut from a white paper doily. Add a loop of string for a hanger.

PINECONE CHRISTMAS TREE
(aluminum foil, construction paper, large paper bag, pinecone)

1. Using scraps of aluminum foil or construction paper, punch out circles with a paper punch, letting them fall into a large paper bag.

2. Brush glue onto a pinecone's "branches." Place the pinecone into the bag of paper circles, close the bag, and shake.

3. Gently remove the decorated cone from the bag, and let it dry.

SANTA'S HELPER
(cardboard egg carton, poster paint, moveable plastic eyes, paper, yarn)

1. Cut two cups from a cardboard egg carton for the body. Cut a pillar for the head and one for the hat. Cut arms and legs from the lid of the carton.

2. Glue the arms and legs in between the two cups and let dry. Paint the body. Add black gloves and boots.

3. Paint one pillar for the head. When dry, glue it to the body. Glue moveable plastic eyes and a paper mouth to the face.

4. Cut the second pillar to fit on top of the head. Paint and glue it in place for the hat.

5. Add a loop of yarn to the back for a hanger.

UNDER-THE-TREE SURPRISE
(quart-size milk carton, paper, tissue paper)

1. Wash and dry a quart-size cardboard milk carton. Measure 2 1/2 inches from the bottom and draw a line around the carton on three sides. Cut on the line and up the sides of the carton, leaving the fourth panel, as shown.

2. Cut a piece of paper the same size as the fourth panel above the 2 1/2-inch base. Draw and cut out a picture of Santa. Glue it to the panel with the open carton in front. Trim around the edges of the drawing.

3. Decorate the bottom of the carton with paper to look like a chimney. Place red tissue paper in the carton. Fill with treats.

Cut shape

2 1/2"

STAINED-GLASS WINDOW
(white shelf paper, crayons, paper towels, cotton balls, baby oil, poster board)

1. Cut a piece of white shelf paper to fit in a window. Sketch a drawing on the panel in pencil. With black crayon, draw heavily over the lines about a quarter of an inch in width, creating the "leading."

2. Color each area within the leading, pressing hard on the crayon to get as deep a color and as opaque a covering as possible.

3. Turn the panel face down on a paper towel-covered surface. Dip a cotton ball in baby oil and rub the back of the paper. The oil gives a translucent effect of stained glass.

4. Wipe off any excess oil and let dry. Cut strips of poster board and glue together to form a frame. Tape the stained-glass picture in the frame.

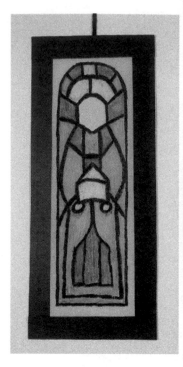

FOIL TASSEL
(aluminum foil, ribbon)

1. Tear a piece of aluminum foil the length you would like the tassel to be.

2. Cut long slits across the width of the foil, leaving a solid band at the top to hold fringe together, as shown.

3. Roll the band around a pencil very carefully. Remove and hold the top of the tassel together. Press the band together and bend the end to form a hook.

4. Decorate the hook with ribbon.

HOLIDAY FLOWER POT
(clay flower pot and base, acrylic paint; high-gloss, waterbased crystal-clear glaze)

1. Cover a clay flower pot and base with an acrylic paint and let dry. Paint on a holiday design.

2. When dry, *ask an adult to help you* cover the flower pot and base with a clear glaze, following the package directions.

PAPER DOILY CARD
(paper, paper doily, self-adhesive stars)

1. Cut and fold a piece of paper to fit a 4-by-9 1/2-inch envelope.

2. Create trees by cutting cone-shaped pieces from paper doilies. Arrange them in a row on the card and glue in place. Add self-adhesive stars and a tree base cut from paper.

3. Write a Christmas greeting inside the card.

• •

CHOIR BOY AND GIRL
(cardboard string spools, paint, two 1 1/2-inch plastic-foam balls, yarn, paper)

1. Cover two cardboard string spools with two coats of paint, letting them dry between coats.

2. Glue a 1 1/2-inch plastic-foam ball to the top of each spool for a head. When dry, spread glue and place pieces of yarn for hair. Add paper eyelids and mouths.

3. Cut and glue long white collars from paper. Add paper bows and hymnals.

• •

SANTA'S HOUSE
(shoe box and lid, construction paper, felt, white cardboard)

1. Cover the outside top and sides of a shoe-box lid with construction paper. Cut a large hole in the top of the lid. Cover the outside of the shoe box with paper.

2. Inside the box, cut and glue white paper to the bottom and the two short sides. Cut and glue felt to one of the long sides to make a rug.

3. Lay the box on its side with the "rug" down. Draw and cut out a window and a door and glue them on the back "wall."

4. Draw and cut out a Santa, Christmas tree, Rudolph, and other objects from white cardboard, leaving a tab at the bottom of each.

Color them. Bend the tabs back and glue them inside Santa's house.

5. Glue the lid on the shoe box and place it on a table for decoration.

Christmas Trees

These tabletop Christmas trees are easy to make. Use them to decorate your home, or give them as gifts.

● ● ● ● ● ● ● ● ● ●

PINECONE TREE
(plastic-foam cone, felt, pinecones, ball ornaments)

1. Cover a plastic-foam cone with felt and let dry.

2. Starting at the bottom of the cone, glue on small pinecones. Continue around the cone, adding some shiny ball ornaments. You may want to let a small section dry before you continue.

3. When you reach the top of the cone, add a larger pinecone.

GLITTER TREE
(poster board, old newspaper, glitter)

1. On a 12-by-18-inch piece of poster board, draw and cut out a large half-circle. Draw four smaller half-circles on it, as shown.

2. Draw and cut out a small V-shape pattern from poster board that will fit between the half-circles. Trace around the pattern, drawing V shapes about an inch apart, all pointing outward. Cut the sides of each V shape to form a small tab.

3. Cover your work area with old newspaper. Squeeze glue on the half-circles and on the tabs. Sprinkle with different colors of glitter and let dry.

4. Shake off the excess glitter and pull the half-circle into a cone shape. Tape or staple the overlap. Bend out the tabs.

● ●

PAPER TREE
(poster board, construction paper, self-adhesive stars)

1. To make the tree trunk, color a piece of white poster board brown, or cut a strip of brown poster board to measure 4 by 27 inches. Fold 2 inches in from each narrow end. Overlap the folded pieces and tape together, forming a triangular shape that will stand.

2. To make tree branches, cut pieces of green construction paper and glue to the trunk. Place self-adhesive stars over the tree. Add a paper star to the top.

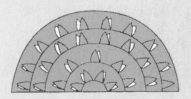

SEQUIN TREE

(lightweight cardboard, felt, rickrack, sequins, ball ornament)

1. Cover both sides of two pieces of lightweight cardboard with green felt. Draw and cut out a Christmas tree from a third piece of lightweight cardboard. Trace around the tree on each felt-covered board and cut them out.

2. On one tree, cut a slit in the center, beginning at the bottom and extending halfway up the tree. The slit width should be slightly more than the thickness of the cardboard. On the second tree, cut a slit in the center, beginning at the top and extending halfway down the tree.

3. Slip the two trees together to form a three-dimensional tree. Add some glue at the seams and let dry.

4. Glue rickrack along the tree edges and let dry. Glue a variety of sequin shapes to decorate the tree. Add a small ball ornament to the top.

TISSUE TREE

(poster board, plastic-foam tray, tissue paper, paper plate)

1. Cut a half-circle from a piece of poster board. Place the half-circle on top of a piece of plastic-foam tray to protect your work area. With a pencil, carefully poke holes through the half-circle, about 1 inch apart. Discard the plastic-foam tray. Roll the half-circle into a cone and staple or tape it together.

2. Cut circles, about 3 inches in diameter, from tissue paper. Pinch the center of one of these circles into a point.

3. Squeeze some glue onto a small paper plate. Place the point of the tissue into the glue and insert it into one of the holes on the cone. Repeat until the whole tree is covered.

RIBBON TREE

(cereal box, construction paper, old ribbon bows)

1. Cut the top flaps from a cereal box. Cut sections from the front and back of the box, as shown.

2. Tape the sides and the triangular sections on the front and back together to form a tree shape. You may need to trim the top points evenly.

3. Lay the different sides of the tree on construction paper and trace around each side. Cut out the traced sections of paper and glue them to the tree.

4. Glue or tape old ribbon bows to the tree.

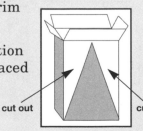

cut out   cut out

SANTA CARDHOLDER
(two 9-inch heavy paper plates, paint, construction paper, cotton balls)

1. Cover the top of one heavy paper plate with red paint and let dry. Cut the other paper plate in half. (Save one half for other crafts.)

2. With the bottom facing upward, place the half plate on top of the painted plate. Staple around the edges, leaving the cut edge open.

3. For the face, cut out construction paper eyes and mouth. Glue these to the plate half. Add cotton balls for the hair, the mustache, and the beard.

4. Add cotton balls to the edge of the red plate to decorate the hat. Glue a yarn loop to the back for a hanger. Fill with cards.

POINSETTIA CARD
(construction paper, glitter)

1. Fold a sheet of construction paper to make a card.

2. Cut out petals from red paper. Glue the petals to the front of the card. Spread glue in the center and sprinkle on gold glitter. Let dry.

3. Shake off the excess glitter. Write a holiday message inside the card.

CHRISTMAS CHAIN
(corrugated cardboard, paint, long sewing needle, string)

1. Cut several 2 1/2-inch circles from corrugated cardboard. Paint the circles, making designs on both sides.

2. When dry, hold them together by threading a long sewing needle with string through the corrugated sections of the cardboard.

3. Hang the chain or tie it to your tree.

FELT ORNAMENT
(felt, rickrack, string of craft pearls, sequins, string)

1. Draw and cut out two identical circles from felt. Glue the circles together.

2. Cut and glue pieces of rickrack, a string of craft pearls, and sequins to decorate.

3. With a paper punch, punch a hole and tie a string for a hanger.

SANTA COOKIE CAN
(cardboard container, construction paper)

1. Use a cardboard container that has a plastic snap-top lid and is at least 3 inches in diameter.

2. Cover the outside of the container with construction paper. Create your Santa with cut pieces of construction paper.

YARN WREATH
(cardboard, yarn, plastic-foam trays, acrylic paint, glitter, ribbon)

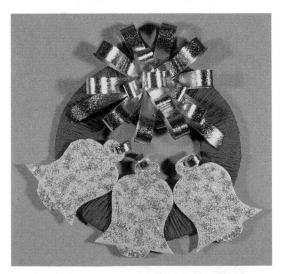

1. To make a wreath, cut a doughnut shape from cardboard about 9 inches in diameter. Tape the starting end of a ball of green yarn to the cardboard. Wrap the yarn around the cardboard until it is covered. Tuck the finished end under the wrapped yarn.

2. Draw and cut out three bells from white plastic-foam trays. Paint the bells with gold and silver acrylic paint. Sprinkle them with gold and silver glitter while the paint is wet and let dry.

3. Make a bow, following directions on page 60, and glue it to the top of the wreath. With a paper punch, punch a hole at the top of each bell and glue a piece of ribbon.

4. Glue the bells to the wreath. Add a piece of yarn to the back of the wreath for a hanger.

EGG-CUP ORNAMENT
(cardboard egg carton, string, paint, glitter)

1. Cut two cups from a cardboard egg carton. Place a string in between the cups and glue the cups together.

2. Paint the ornament and sprinkle with glitter. Let dry.

• •

RED BERRIES
(paper towel tube, paint, string)

1. Cut 1-inch rings from a paper towel tube. Paint the inside and outside of three rings with red paint and let dry. Paint two rings green and let dry.

2. Glue the three red rings together, forming berries. Press the green rings together to form leaves and glue them to the berries. Hold the rings in place with paper clips if needed.

3. Glue a loop of string in between the leaves for a hanger.

HOBBYHORSE
(old sock, rags, wooden dowel, heavy-duty tape, large-eyed needle, heavy thread, ribbon, silver buttons, D rings, bells, black buttons, felt, yarn)

1. Stuff an old sock with rags. Put one end of a wooden dowel into the sock as far as the heel. Stuff rags around the dowel, then tape the end of the sock to the dowel.

2. Using a large-eyed needle and heavy thread, sew pieces of ribbon to make the bridle. (You may want to *ask an adult to help you.*) Sew on silver buttons for decoration. Sew two D rings to the ends of the ribbon near the mouth area for the bit ends. Sew each end of a long piece of ribbon to the D rings for the reins. Sew bells to the reins.

3. Sew on two black buttons for eyes, adding pieces of felt for details. Sew two felt ears and a blaze in place. Glue pieces of felt to make the nostrils, mouth, and tongue of the horse.

4. To make the mane, cut pieces of yarn 2 to 3 inches in length. Tie four to six pieces together in the middle with another piece of yarn. Sew the center of each bunch to the sock. Sew one bunch between the ears for the forelock.

EASY TREE CARD
(poster board, construction paper)

1. Cut a piece of poster board 7 by 8 inches. Fold it so the card is 4 by 7 inches.

2. From construction paper of two different colors, cut triangles of different sizes. Arrange them to form tree shapes.

3. Cut a paper base for the tree. Glue the base and the triangles, creating a tree shape on the front of the card.

• •

"GINGERBREAD" CHARACTERS
(light brown paper)

1. Cut a strip of light brown paper about 18 by 3 1/2 inches. Fold one end of the strip to make a rectangle about 2 1/2 by 3 1/2 inches. Fold the rest of the strip back and forth under the first rectangle, making each section the same size as the first.

2. On the first rectangle, draw a gingerbread character with the hands touching the folds and the legs reaching the bottom of the paper.

3. Keeping the paper folded, cut out the character. Do not cut through the folded paper at the end of the hands. Unfold the paper.

4. The characters should be in a row, holding hands. Decorate them with markers.

DEER FINGER PUPPET
(old brown cotton glove, paper, ribbon)

1. To make the puppet, cut off a finger from an old brown cotton glove. With a paper punch, punch out two white paper dots for eyes and a red paper dot for the nose. Glue these to one side of the fingertip to form the facial features.

2. From light brown paper, cut out antlers and glue them to the back of the fingertip. Make a bow tie from a piece of ribbon and paper, and glue in place.

3. Place your finger in the glove finger, and work your deer puppet.

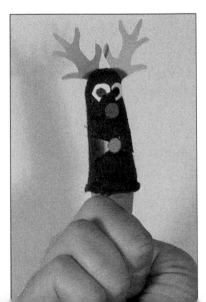

CHRISTMAS ANGEL
(construction paper, tinsel garland)

1. From construction paper, cut a head, a body, arms, hands, and wings. Place the pieces on a table to form an angel, and staple all the pieces together.

2. Draw hair, eyes, a nose, and a mouth on the face. Add pieces of tinsel garland for a halo and on the bottom of the angel's skirt.

3. Attach a piece of yarn at the top to hang the angel on a wall or in a window.

STAR GLUE ORNAMENT
(cardboard, plastic wrap, white glue, yarn, paper plate, food coloring)

1. Draw the outline of a star with a loop on a piece of cardboard. Place a piece of plastic wrap on top. Squeeze white glue on the outline. Press two strands of yarn in the glue.

2. On a paper plate, mix a few drops of food coloring with white glue. Pour the colored glue inside the star design. Dry for several days.

3. Peel the star from the plastic wrap and hang it on your tree.

PINECONE CANDLE HOLDER
(corrugated cardboard, felt, decorative trim, small wooden candle holder, pinecones, ball ornaments, candle)

1. Cut a 5-inch circle from corrugated cardboard. Trace around the circle on red felt. Cut out the felt circle and glue it on top of the cardboard. Add decorative trim around the edge.

2. Glue a small wooden candle holder in the center. Glue pinecones around the candle holder along with ball ornaments.

3. Place a candle in the holder.

BELL NECKLACE
(empty thread spools, fabric, bells, cording)

1. Place thread spool ends on fabric and trace around them with a pencil. Cut out the circles of fabric and glue them on the spool ends. Cut an X through the center holes.

2. Glue fabric around the spools and let dry.

3. Thread the spools and bells on a piece of cording long enough to hang loosely around your neck. Tie a bow at the ends.

CHRISTMAS-TREE GAME
(two white poster boards, plastic lids)

1. Tape two white poster boards together end to end on one side. Turn the boards over. Using a yardstick and pencil, draw a tree shape, including its trunk.

2. Divide the tree into sections using a black marker. Draw a number in each section. Color the tree green, leaving the numbers white. Color the trunk brown.

3. Place the tree on the floor. Give each player a turn at throwing three plastic lids on the playing board. Total each player's score after three throws. See who can get the highest number of points.

NORTH POLE EXPRESS
(individual-sized cereal boxes, construction paper, plastic tops, cardboard, string)

1. Close the flaps of individual-sized cereal boxes with tape. Cover with glue and construction paper.

2. Decorate the car and caboose with paper windows. Draw children looking out. Add a sign that says "North Pole Express." Decorate the engine with paper windows. Add the engineers.

3. Glue various types of plastic tops to the engine and caboose. Cut out cardboard wheels and glue them to the train.

4. Attach the cars together with pieces of string and glue.

HOLLY DECORATION
(green poster board, paper, cording)

1. From green poster board, cut out five holly leaves. Outline their edges with a marker. Glue the leaves together to form a body.

2. Cut out a circle and glue it to the body for the head. Cut out a holly leaf, outline its edge, and glue it in place for a hat.

3. From paper, add facial features, berries on the hat, and red circles near the hands and feet. Attach a loop of cording at the back to hang the decoration.

CRÈCHE TREE ORNAMENT
(three ice-cream sticks, brown shoe polish, paper, string)

1. Rub three ice-cream sticks with brown shoe polish. Glue the sticks together to form a triangle.

2. Cut colorful pieces of paper, and glue them together to create Joseph, Mary, and the Christ Child in a manger. Add details with a marker. Glue the family to the bottom of the triangle.

3. Attach a piece of string to the back.

HOLIDAY PLACE MAT
(poster board, construction paper, clear self-adhesive paper)

1. Cut a piece of white poster board the same size as a large sheet of construction paper. Gently fold the construction paper in half and cut around the inside to form a curved frame. Glue the frame on top of the poster board.

2. On the poster board, draw a picture and write a holiday greeting with colored markers.

3. Cut a piece of clear self-adhesive paper a little larger than the place mat. *Ask an adult to help you* separate the adhesive paper from its backing. Cover the front of the place mat and overlap the edges.

4. Keep the place mat clean with a damp cloth.

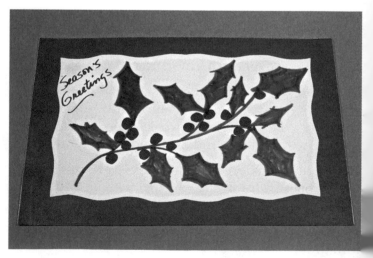

SILVER BELLS
(cardboard egg cartons, acrylic paint, glitter, string, bells)

1. To make the bell shapes, cut three pillars from a cardboard egg carton. Cover them inside and out with acrylic paint. Sprinkle them with glitter and let dry.

2. Attach a string to a metal bell and tie a knot about an inch above it.

3. Poke a small hole in the cardboard bell and pull the string through the hole until the knot is against the inside of the cardboard bell. Tie a knot in the string on top of the cardboard bell.

4. Follow step 2 and 3 for the other two bells. Gather all the strings together and tie a knot. Hang the bells in a window or on a door.

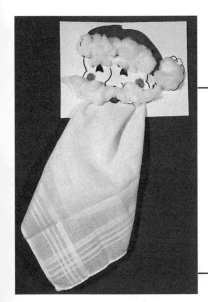

SANTA HANKY
(poster board, cotton balls, white handkerchief)

1. Draw and paint a Santa face on a 6-by-8-inch piece of poster board. Make a cut along the bottom of the moustache. Add cotton balls to the hat, eyebrows, and moustache.

2. Fold a white handkerchief in half. Make pleats along the fold, and insert half of the handkerchief in the slit under the moustache.

ADVENT CENTERPIECE
(corrugated cardboard, paper, felt, rickrack, five bathroom tissue tubes, pompons)

1. To make the base for the centerpiece, cut an 8-inch circle from corrugated cardboard. Lay the base on a piece of paper, trace around it, and cut it out. Do the same with a piece of white felt. Glue the paper and then the felt on top of the base. Glue rickrack around the edge.

2. To make the candles, cut and glue purple felt around three bathroom tissue tubes. Glue light purple felt on one tube and red felt on another. Glue the tubes to the base.

3. Decorate around the candle bases with holly leaves cut from green felt. Add red pompons for berries. Cut pieces of yellow felt for the candle flames. Roll pieces of tape to attach a flame to each appropriate candle.

(Attach a flame to one purple candle for each of the three Sundays before Christmas. Light the light purple one on the fourth Sunday. Light the red candle on Christmas Day.)

MOUSE RIBBON HOLDER
(paper towel tube, cardboard, felt)

1. For the body, cut a piece of gray felt and glue it around a paper towel tube. Cut the head and ear shapes from cardboard. Cover both sides with felt. Glue the head to one end of the tube with the ears in between. Let dry.

2. Draw and cut legs and feet from cardboard. Cover both sides with felt. Glue them in place on the body.

3. For the tail, cut a long, thin piece of felt and glue it in place.

4. Wrap loose ribbon around the body of the mouse and tape the end securely until needed.

FOLDED BELL CARD
(construction paper, ribbon)

1. Cut two pieces of white construction paper about 3 inches square. Fold them in half. Draw a half bell at the folded edge. Cut out the two bells.

2. Using a paper punch, hold the bells together and punch a hole at the top of the bells. Tie the bells together with a piece of ribbon. Write a message on the top bell.

3. Cut a piece of construction paper 9 by 5 inches. Fold it in half to 4 1/2 by 5 inches.

4. Glue the back of the bottom bell to the center of the card. Glue only the fold line of the top bell to the bottom bell, making a three-dimensional effect.

GROCERY BAG STOCKING
(large brown paper bag, yarn, paper)

1. Cut down the seam of a large brown paper bag and cut out the bottom. Cut out two stocking shapes from the paper.

2. Hold the two stockings together and punch holes about 1 inch apart. Lace the two stockings together with yarn. Make a loop at the end.

3. Cut white paper for the stocking cuff. Write a name on it, and glue it to the top of the stocking. Decorate the rest of the stocking with a snowman or other holiday figure.

TABLE ANGEL
(bathroom tissue tube, gold gift wrap,
2-inch plastic-foam ball, lightweight cardboard,
glitter, tinsel garland, cotton ball, paper)

1. For the body, cover a bathroom tissue tube with gold gift wrap. For the head, glue a 2-inch plastic-foam ball on one end of the tube and let dry.

2. Draw and cut out wings from lightweight cardboard, as shown. Glue gold gift wrap to each side of the wings, and trim the edges with scissors. Add dabs of glue, sprinkle with glitter, and let dry. Glue the wings to the body.

3. For the base, draw and cut out a 6-inch circle from heavy cardboard and cover it with gold gift wrap. Glue the body to the base. Add tinsel garland for decoration.

4. For hair, glue on pieces of a cotton ball. Add cut-paper facial features.

5. For a halo, cover a small piece of lightweight cardboard on both sides with gold gift wrap. Cut out a small strip and a circle. Cut the center from the circle. Glue the halo to the strip. Glue the strip to the back of the angel.

CUTOUT ORNAMENT
(bathroom tissue tube, poster paint, string)

1. Using a paper punch, punch holes around each end of a bathroom tissue tube in a decorative pattern. Cut out small oval sections within the tube.

2. Cover the tube with poster paint. Decorate with another color and let dry. Tie a string to the ornament and hang on your Christmas tree.

FABRIC WALL DECORATION
(fabric, embroidery hoop, rickrack, cardboard, cotton batting)

1. Place a piece of fabric in an embroidery hoop. Trim around the edge. Glue rickrack around the rim of the hoop and let dry.

2. Cut pieces of cardboard to form a house shape that will fit inside the hoop area.

3. Glue one layer of cotton batting on top of the cardboard pieces. Cut fabric a little larger than the cardboard pieces, and wrap it around the cardboard. Glue the extra fabric to the back.

4. Glue the house to the fabric in the hoop. Decorate with pieces of fabric to make windows and a door. Add rickrack to the roof.

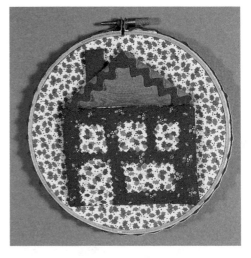

YARN HOLIDAY CARD
(construction paper, yarn)

1. Fold a piece of construction paper in half to make a card.

2. On the front of the card, draw the outline of the design you want.

3. Squeeze glue on the outline. Press yarn into the glue and let it dry.

4. Write a holiday greeting inside.

STRING ORNAMENT
(white glue, water, disposable container, balloon, string, glitter)

1. Mix equal amounts of white glue and water in a disposable container.

2. Blow up a small round balloon and knot the end. Tie a piece of string around the knot.

3. Dip pieces of string into the glue mixture. Wrap the strings around the inflated balloon. Sprinkle on some glitter and let dry.

4. Pop the balloon and pull it out from between the strings.

PAPER PINECONES
(brown paper bag, white paint, yarn)

1. Cut a square from a brown paper bag. Roll it tightly around a pencil and fasten the rolled-up paper with tape. Remove the pencil.

2. Cut many oval-shaped pieces from the same paper bag. Curl one end of each over a closed pair of scissors. Glue them to the rolled paper, starting at one end. Glue on more rows, overlapping each row, until the roll is covered.

3. Brush a little white paint at the tip of each scale to look like snow. Add a yarn loop to the top of the cone, and hang on your Christmas tree.

BELL PICTURE FRAME
(paper, photograph, plastic-foam tray, acrylic paint, decorative trim)

1. Draw and cut out a bell shape from paper, large enough for the photograph you have selected. Trace the bell pattern on a plastic-foam tray and cut it out. Cut out an oval shape in the center of the bell to fit the photograph.

2. Paint the bell with an acrylic paint and let dry. Cut a small tab from another plastic-foam tray. Paint it and let dry.

3. Tie a bow of decorative trim and glue to the top of the bell. Glue some trim around the oval opening.

4. Tape your photo to the back of the frame, centering the picture in the oval. Tape the tab to the back so the frame will stand.

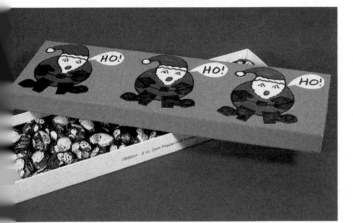

SANTA CANDY BOX
(paper, empty candy box)

1. Cut and glue bright paper to the top of an empty candy box.

2. Draw and cut out a Santa pattern from white paper. Trace around the pattern on white paper, making two more Santas. Cut out the Santas and color them with markers.

3. Glue the Santas on the box top. Cut out three white caption balloons and write "Ho!" in each one. Glue one next to each Santa.

HOLLY NAPKIN RINGS
(empty adhesive-tape rings, ribbon, felt)

1. Cover the outside of empty adhesive-tape rings with glue and ribbon.

2. Cut holly leaves and berries from felt. Glue them to the rings.

3. Place a napkin in each ring for your dinner guests.

MILK-CARTON CHURCH
(half-gallon milk carton, white tape, construction paper)

1. Wash and dry an empty half-gallon milk carton. Staple the top closed. Cover the carton with pieces of white tape.

2. To make the roof, cut out two pieces of black construction paper and glue to each side of the top of the carton, extending a little over the edge. Cut small slits along the edge.

3. To make windows, cut shapes from black paper. Fold them and cut out little sections. Unfold and glue pieces of different-colored paper over the cutout sections. Glue the windows in place on the church.

4. Cut a door from red paper and add black trim. Draw a cross on black paper. Cut it out and glue it to the top.

ACTION CARD
(poster board, plastic lid, yarn)

1. Draw an outdoor scene on a 3-by-4-inch piece of white poster board. On another piece of poster board, the same size, draw lots of fluffy snowflakes.

2. Glue a 1-by-2-inch piece of plastic lid to the middle of the back of each card to add weight so it will spin.

3. Cut a 36-inch piece of yarn, double it, and knot the ends. Find the middle of the doubled yarn, and glue it to the plastic on the back of the snowflake card.

4. Glue the cards together with the pictures outside and the yarn extending from the right and left sides. Print a greeting on the card and sign your name.

5. Place a note in with your card that says "Wind card by holding the ends of the yarn and spinning the card. Firmly pull ends of yarn away from the card and watch snowflakes fall on the scene."

FABRIC ORNAMENT
(fabric, 2 1/2-inch plastic-foam ball, yarn)

1. Cut 1-inch squares from scraps of different-colored fabric.

2. Place a small drop of glue on a plastic-foam ball. Center a fabric square over the glue. Push the fabric into the ball with a dull-pointed pencil. Repeat until the ball is covered.

3. Knot the ends of a 6-inch piece of yarn together. Place glue on the knot, and push it into the ball between two pieces of fabric. Let dry.

SANTA'S SNACK TRAY
(9-inch-round aluminum tin, gift wrap, clear self-adhesive paper, ribbon, paper)

1. Trace around the outside of a 9-inch-round aluminum tin on a piece of gift wrap and a piece of clear self-adhesive paper. Cut out the circles.

2. First glue the gift-wrap circle in the tin. Then you may want to *ask an adult to help you* separate the adhesive paper from its backing and place the adhesive-paper circle on top of the gift wrap.

3. Glue a piece of ribbon around the outer edge of the aluminum tin. Add a ribbon bow. Staple a paper note that says "To Santa" on the edge.

4. Fill the tin with cookies and milk for Santa on Christmas Eve.

SANTA PUPPET
(round cardboard food container, felt, cotton balls)

1. Wash and dry a round cardboard food container such as one in which snacks are packaged.

2. To make the head, measure the container and cut a piece of felt to fit around it. Glue the felt in place.

3. To make the hat, cut out a circle of red felt larger in diameter than the container. Turn the container upside down so the bottom faces upward. Spread glue around the outside bottom edge. Place the edge of the felt in the glue, gathering the felt together if needed. Hold in place with a rubber band and let dry.

4. Glue a cotton ball to the top of the hat, and add some around the bottom. Make eyes, a nose, and a mouth from felt. Attach them with glue. Add cotton balls for hair, a beard, and a moustache.

5. Place your arm and hand inside the container to move your puppet.

HOLIDAY ACTIVITY BOARD
(heavy corrugated cardboard, gift wrap, ribbon, cording)

1. Cut two 12-inch squares from heavy corrugated cardboard. Glue or tape them together. Cover the cardboard with gift wrap, taping the extra paper on the back like a package.

2. Glue ribbon around the front and the back of the board. Let dry.

3. *Ask an adult to help you* poke two holes at the top of the board. Thread a piece of cording through the holes to hang the activity board.

HEART ORNAMENT
(cookie cutter, cardboard, acrylic paint; dried beans, peas, and barley, string)

1. Place a heart-shaped cookie cutter on a piece of cardboard and trace around it with a pencil. Cut out the heart.

2. Paint both sides of the heart with acrylic paint and let dry. Use a paper punch to punch a hole near the top of the heart.

3. Glue different kinds of dried beans, peas, and barley on one side of the heart. Let dry.

4. Place a loop of string through the hole to hang the ornament on your tree.

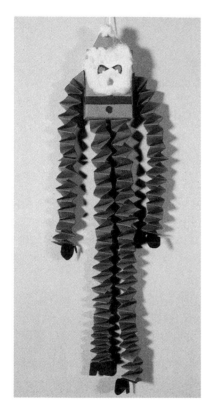

BOUNCING SANTA
(individual-sized cereal box, construction paper, cotton balls, yarn)

1. Close the flaps of an individual-sized cereal box with tape. Cover with glue and red construction paper.

2. Add a triangle of red paper for the hat. Add facial features with paper. Glue cotton balls for hair, a beard, and a moustache.

3. Cut long strips of red paper and fold, as shown, to make arms and legs that will spring. Glue in place. Add boots and mittens from black paper.

4. Glue a yarn loop at the top of the head behind the hat. Let dry. Jiggle the loop, and watch Santa jiggle like a bowl full of jelly.

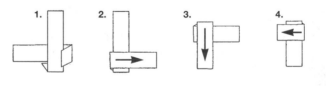

HOLIDAY HUMMER
(gift wrap, cardboard tube, waxed paper, rubber band, pen or pencil)

1. Glue gift wrap around a 4 1/2-inch cardboard tube.

2. Cut a 4-inch-square piece of waxed paper. Place it over one end of the tube and hold it in place with a rubber band.

3. *Ask an adult to help you* make two or three holes along the side of the tube, using a pen or pencil.

4. Hum into the open end of the tube, and "play" the hummer by covering and uncovering the holes with your fingers.

RIBBON BARRETTE
(3-inch metal barrette base, cardboard, ribbon, bell)

1. Recycle an old metal barrette base by removing the old ribbon.

2. Cut a 3-inch-long piece of cardboard the width of your ribbon. Glue an 8-inch-long piece of red ribbon around it, gluing the ends underneath. Glue the cardboard to the top of the barrette. Hold it in place with rubber bands and let dry.

3. Cut three 8-inch pieces of ribbon. Glue the ends of each ribbon together to form three loops. Glue the center of each loop to the center of the barrette, as shown. Let dry.

4. Glue a bell to the center of the ribbon loops. You may need to tape the bell lightly to hold in place until the glue dries.

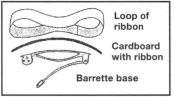

Loop of ribbon

Cardboard with ribbon

Barrette base

PAPER-PUNCH CARD
(construction paper)

1. Fold a piece of construction paper to form a small card. Cut a holiday design from a piece of paper and glue it to the front of the card.

2. Use a paper punch to punch dots from different-colored paper. Arrange them on the holiday design and glue in place.

3. Write a message inside.

THREE WISE MEN
(paper, gift wrap, self-adhesive stars, bottle cap, lipstick tube top, cardboard)

1. Draw two 10-inch paper circles. Cut them in half. Glue three half-circles into cone shapes for the gowns, leaving a small opening at the top.

2. From paper, cut three heads with long necks. Add eyes and mouths. Stick the necks into the cones and tape underneath. Cut arms from paper and glue to the sides.

3. Make collars by cutting small circles of gift wrap. Cut a small hole in the center and a slit from the outside edge to the center hole. Slip the collars over the heads and glue in place.

4. Cut and glue pieces of gift wrap to make crowns and to decorate the gowns. Add self-adhesive stars.

5. To make the gifts, glue a bottle cap, a lipstick tube top, and cardboard covered in gift wrap to the ends of the arms. Add stars.

THE CHIMNEY GAME
(paper, plastic berry basket, string, Santa ornament)

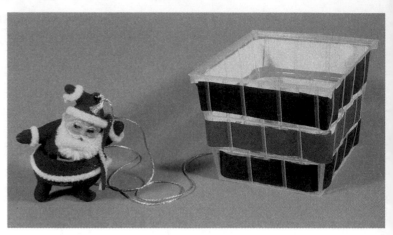

1. To make the chimney, cut strips of paper to weave in and out through sections of a plastic berry basket. Overlap the ends and glue together.

2. Attach a piece of string from the outside bottom of the basket to a non-breakable Santa ornament.

3. Hold the chimney in your hands and try to swing Santa into the chimney.

HOLIDAY BANNER
(felt, fabric glue, wooden dowel, decorative trim)

1. Place four pieces of felt vertically. Overlap the edges about 1 inch and glue together with fabric glue. Fold the top edge of the first panel over a small wooden dowel and glue in place. Let dry.

2. Cut Christmas symbols such as a candle, a bell, a tree, and a dove from pieces of felt and glue onto the panels.

3. Glue or staple decorative trim around the ends of the dowel for a hanger.

MISTLETOE BALL
(3-inch plastic-foam ball, lace, ribbon, plastic mistletoe, straight pin)

1. Place a 3-inch plastic-foam ball in the center of a 14-inch circle of lace.

2. Gather the lace around the ball and tie a piece of ribbon tightly to hold the lace together. Make loops from a second piece of ribbon and attach them to the first ribbon, making a knot. Leave the ribbon ends loose.

3. Poke pieces of plastic mistletoe in between the holes of the lace. Add glue to hold the leaves in position if necessary.

4. To make a hanger, cut a long piece of ribbon. Place a straight pin through the ends. Push the pin into the top of the ball.

PERSONALIZED SLED
(ice-cream sticks, cardboard, paint, paper, string)

1. Glue five ice-cream sticks together for the sled frame. Cut a piece of cardboard to look like a short ice-cream stick, and glue it to the sled for the handles.

2. Glue two ice-cream sticks to the bottom of the sled for runners.

3. Paint the sled and let dry. Add your name with paint and let dry. Add paper gloves and boots. Glue a piece of string for a hanger.

BAG-IT SNOWMAN
(plastic-mesh vegetable bag, cotton balls, string, ribbon, cardboard, paint, 35mm plastic film canister, paper, button, twigs)

1. Fill a plastic-mesh vegetable bag with cotton balls. Gather at the top and tie a piece of string to hold closed. Tie a piece of ribbon around the center, forming a head and a body.

2. To make a hat, cut and paint a small circle of cardboard. Then glue a black 35mm plastic film canister on top. Glue the hat in place.

3. Add paper eyes and a button nose. Cut out paper boots and glue in place. Add twigs for arms.

THE NORTH POLE
(two rectangular tissue boxes, construction paper, poster board, one individual-sized cereal box, one toothpaste box, cotton balls)

1. To make the house shape, tape together two rectangular tissue boxes. Cover them with construction paper.

2. To make the roof, fold a piece of poster board in half. Cut it the same width as the house. Tape one edge of the roof to one side of the box and tape the other edge to the other side. To make the sides of the roof, place the side of the house on a piece of poster board and trace around the open area. Cut out the shape and tape it in place. Do the same to the other side.

3. Cut several 1-inch strips of black paper. Cut slits along one edge. Glue the uncut edges of the strips to the roof. Bend the slits up slightly to look like shingles.

4. To make the chimney, cover an individual-sized cereal box and a toothpaste box with paper. Glue it to the side of the house. Draw bricks on the chimney and stones on the house.

5. Add cut-paper windows, a door, signs, and icicles. To make snow, pull sections from cotton balls and glue across the roof, chimney, and the front of the house.

HOLIDAY BOOKMARK
(plain ribbon, plaid ribbon, old greeting card)

1. Glue a narrow piece of plain ribbon on top of a wide piece of plaid ribbon about 10 inches long. Cut a V shape from each end.

2. Cut a holiday scene from an old greeting card and glue it on top of the ribbons. Let dry.

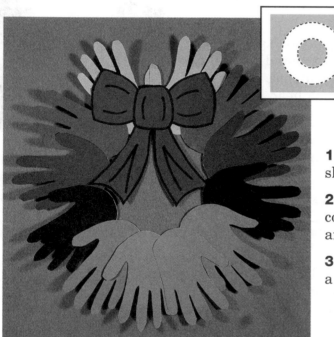

HAND WREATH
(10-inch and 6-inch plates, poster board, construction paper, yarn)

1. Trace around a 10-inch and a 6-inch plate, as shown. Cut out the circles, making a doughnut shape.

2. Trace around your hand on different-colored construction paper. Cut out the hands. Glue the hands around the doughnut.

3. Add a paper bow. Glue a loop of yarn to the back for a hanger.

SNOW-JAR PAPERWEIGHT
(baby-food jar, plastic or ceramic ornament, adhesive cement, water, glitter, ribbon)

1. Wash and dry an empty baby-food jar. Select a small plastic or ceramic Christmas ornament to fit inside the jar. *Ask an adult to help you* glue the ornament to the center of the underside of the lid with an adhesive cement. Let dry overnight.

2. Add water to the jar, almost filling it. Add some glitter. Place the lid tightly on the jar. Glue ribbon around the lid.

3. Turn the jar upside down and watch the snow fall.

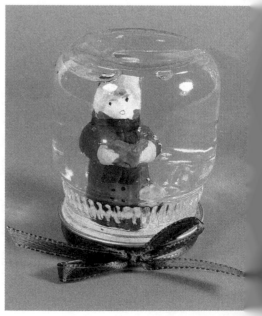

KITCHEN-SPOON ELF
(wooden spoon, paint, felt, sequins, decorative trim, yarn)

1. To make the face, cover the inside of a wooden spoon with paint and let dry. Add eyes, a nose, and a mouth from felt. Add sequins to the eyes.

2. Cut a felt hat and glue to the top of the head. Add pieces of yarn for hair.

3. Using decorative trim, tie a bow around the spoon, under the chin. Add a felt body and hands.

4. Add a loop of yarn to the back and hang the elf in your kitchen.

MOUSE'S HOUSE DOORSTOP
(stones, large cereal box, construction paper)

1. Place some stones inside a large cereal box for weight. Tape the top flaps closed.

2. Cover the box with construction paper. Draw and cut out a mouse hole from black paper and glue in place. Draw and cut out a mouse and glue in front of the door.

3. Add a sign decorated with pieces of holly cut from paper. Write "Mouse's House" on the sign.

4. Place the doorstop by your front door.

BELL-CLUSTER ORNAMENT
(ribbon, bells)

1. Cut a piece of green ribbon about 14 inches long and fold in half. Measure 2 inches down from the fold, and glue the rest of the ribbon together, leaving the 2-inch loop at the top.

2. Tie a knot about 2 inches up from the bottom of the ribbon.

3. Cut four pieces of red ribbon. String one bell on each piece of ribbon, and tie in a bow to the green ribbon above the knot.

4. Slide the bells down to the knot, forming a cluster.

WOODEN BLOCK ORNAMENT
(wooden block, acrylic paint, string)

1. Using a pencil, draw features on a small wooden block to represent a house.

2. Paint the house. Add details such as candles and ribbons to the windows.

3. Form a piece of string into a loop and glue it onto the top of the house for a hanger. You can write the date and your name on the bottom of the ornament.

WINTER SCENE
(paint, heavy paper plate, construction paper, string)

1. Paint the inside and outer edge of a heavy paper plate, making the background for a scene.

2. Cut a snowman, hat, and scarf from construction paper. Glue them onto the scene. Cut tiny pieces of white paper for the snowflakes and glue them around the outer edge of the plate.

3. Glue or tape a loop of string to the back for a hanger.

CHRISTMAS GREENS BASKET
(cardboard box lid, construction paper, greens, pinecones)

1. Cover the inside of a shallow box lid with red construction paper. Cut holly leaves from green paper and glue them onto the sides and the handle. Add red paper berries.

2. Fill the basket with greens and pinecones.

TUBE SURPRISE
(bathroom tissue tube, tissue paper, candies, ribbon, stickers)

1. Cover a bathroom tissue tube with tissue paper that is wider than the tube. Stuff little candies inside.

2. Gather the tissue at each end of the tube and tie with several pieces of different-colored ribbon.

3. Add stickers to the outside for decoration.

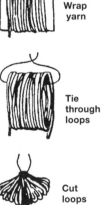

Wrap yarn

Tie through loops

Cut loops

SNOWMAN HAT
(cardboard, yarn, needle and thread, knit cap, moveable plastic eyes, fabric glue, felt)

1. Cut a piece of cardboard 1 1/2 by 2 inches. Wrap white yarn around it, as shown, about forty-five times, or more for a fuller pompon.

2. Carefully slip the yarn from the cardboard, and tie a piece of yarn tightly through the loops. Cut through the loops at the other end. Fluff up the yarn.

3. Sew the white pompon to the cuff of a knit cap. Sew or glue moveable plastic eyes in place. Add a felt hat and a mouth.

DOVE CARD
(poster board, plastic-foam trays, construction paper)

1. Fold a piece of poster board 8 1/4 by 10 3/4 inches in half to form a card.

2. Draw and cut out a dove pattern from paper. Place it on a plastic-foam tray. Trace around the pattern with a pencil, and cut out the dove. Do this again, but turn the pattern over first.

3. Have the doves face each other on the front of the card and glue in place. Add paper holly leaves and berries.

4. Write a holiday message inside.

CORNUCOPIA
(old greeting card, paper clip, paper doily, ribbon)

1. Use an old greeting card and cut the card 6 inches square with the corners at the center top, bottom, and sides of the picture.

2. Roll into a cone. Glue down the long edge, using a paper clip to hold in place.

3. Fold a paper doily in half. Roll it into a cone and place inside the card. Dab some glue around the inside edges to hold the doily in place.

4. With a paper punch, punch a hole at the back of the cone and insert a narrow ribbon as a hanger. Place small gifts or treats in the cornucopia, and hang the decoration on a doorknob or tree.

MATCH-MAKING GAME
(frozen-juice pull-top lids, gift wrap, resealable sandwich bag)

1. Clean the metal lids from several frozen-juice containers.

2. Decorate one side of two lids so they match, using paper cutouts from gift wrap. Decorate the remaining lids in pairs so that each lid has a match.

3. To play, turn the lids facedown. Each player turns over two lids at a time, trying to find a match. The player with the most matches wins.

4. Store the game in a resealable sandwich bag.

CANDY CANE FOREST
(floral foam block, gift wrap, ribbon, cellophane-covered candy canes, cotton balls, paper)

1. Cover a floral foam block with gift wrap. Tape two pieces of ribbon around the sides for decoration.

2. With a pencil, gently poke holes in various places on the foam block. Insert cellophane-covered candy canes in the holes.

3. To make snowmen, glue two cotton balls on top of each other. Add paper eyes, a mouth, and a hat to each one. Glue them near the candy canes.

4. Place the decoration on a table. Replace the candy canes as they are eaten.

HOLIDAY RECIPE BOX
(medium-weight cardboard box, construction paper, cookie cutters)

1. Cut a small section from a medium-weight cardboard box, as shown. The box should be able to hold 4-by-6-inch index cards.

2. Cover the outside of the box with construction paper.

3. Place cookie cutters on colored paper. Trace around the cookie designs. Cut out the designs and glue them on the box.

4. Decorate the designs with paper and markers. Write "Holiday Recipes" on the front of the box.

Cut

DECORATIONS FOR THE BIRDS
(large-eyed needle, string, unsalted popcorn, unsalted unshelled peanuts, wire, yarn, dog biscuits, cookie cutter, stale bread, plastic straw, outdoor tree)

1. With a large-eyed needle and string, thread popped popcorn, making a long garland.

2. Using the needle, thread about twelve unshelled peanuts on a 15-inch piece of wire. Twist the ends together, forming a clothes hanger-like hook. Cut the excess wire.

3. Tie a piece of yarn around one end of a dog biscuit, leaving a loop for a hanger. Make several.

4. Using a cookie cutter, cut shapes from stale bread slices. Make a hole at the top with a plastic straw, and thread a yarn loop for a hanger.

5. Hang the garland, peanuts, dog biscuits, and bread ornaments on an outdoor tree for the birds to eat. Add a bow to the top.

RECTANGLE SANTA CLAUS
(construction paper, cotton balls)

1. Cut two large and two small rectangles from red construction paper.

2. Glue or staple these together so that the two larger rectangles hang down for Santa's legs and the smaller rectangles stick out on each side for his arms.

3. Cut a head and hands from construction paper and attach them in place. Give Santa a red hat and black boots and belt.

4. Draw his face, then give him a cotton-ball beard. Trim his suit and hat with cotton balls.

REINDEER SOCK PUPPET
(paper, spring-type clothespins, sock, pompon, ribbon, bell)

1. To make the antlers, trace around your hands on paper. Cut out the antlers and add details with markers. Glue each to a spring-type clothespin.

2. Lay an old sock on a table. Cut out eyes, eyelashes, and a mouth with a tongue from paper. Glue them to the bottom of the sock. Add a red pompon for a nose.

3. Glue a ribbon with a bell on the leg area of the sock. Place your hand inside the sock, and clip on the antlers at the heel of the sock.

HOLIDAY "COOKIE" MOBILE
(two tongue depressors, bead, string, cookie cutters, poster board)

1. Glue two tongue depressors together at the center. Add a bead at the center. Let dry. Place a string loop through the bead.

2. Trace around cookie-cutter shapes on poster board, making two of each shape. Cut them out. With a paper punch, punch a hole in the top of each shape. Color the shapes with markers.

3. Tie a string from each shape to a tongue depressor. If you hang the same shapes opposite each other, using the same length of string, the mobile will be easier to balance.

PAPER BAG VILLAGE
(paper bags, poster board)

1. Cut 2-inch slits along the four corners of the open ends of brown and white paper bags. When those 2 inches are turned out flat, the bags will stand upright.

2. Flatten each bag again and draw windows and doors on the bags. Make houses, apartment buildings, or stores. Add Christmas decorations to the buildings.

3. Glue the bags to a large piece of poster board. Add streets, sidewalks, lawns, shrubs, cars, and people.

CHRISTMAS CARD ADDRESS BOOK
(cardboard, index cards, fabric, ribbon)

1. To make the front and the back of the book, cut two pieces of cardboard 6 1/2 by 4 1/2 inches. Using a paper punch, punch a hole 1 1/2 inches in from the long sides and 3/4 inch in from the narrow sides, as shown.

2. To make the inside pages, place a 4-by-6-inch index card over the cardboard and mark the holes on the card. Place this card on top of several other cards, and punch out the holes. Create more inside pages, making sure all holes line up.

3. Cut holiday fabric to cover one side of the front and back cardboard pieces. Tape the edges on the other side. Feel the holes in the cardboard underneath the fabric, and punch out the holes.

Trim with scissors. Glue a punched card over the taped fabric, lining up the holes.

4. Place the cards inside the covers. Thread a piece of ribbon through the holes in the back cover, the cards, and the front cover. Tie the ribbon into a bow.

SNOWMAN ORNAMENT
(three plastic beverage caps, poster board, paper, string)

1. Glue three white plastic beverage caps in a row onto a piece of poster board and let dry. Trim around the edges with scissors.

2. Add paper features to make a snowman. Glue a string to the back for a hanger.

ANGEL PLACE CARD
(paper, self-adhesive stars, ribbon, two plastic-foam cups)

1. To make the angel wings, cut a piece of paper 4 inches square. Make accordion pleats, as shown. Dab glue along the center within the folds, and press together.

2. To make the body, cut a piece of paper 4 by 6 inches and pleat parallel to the 6-inch side of the paper. Dab glue about 2 inches from one end within the folds, and press together.

3. Glue the wings to the body. Cut out a paper circle for the head and glue in place. Add self-adhesive stars for a halo. Cut out paper eyes and a mouth. Tie a ribbon around the waist. Glue an ice-cream stick to the back of the angel and let dry.

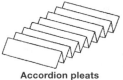

Accordion pleats

4. Place one plastic-foam cup inside another and glue together. Add a ribbon around the rim. Cut a small slit in the bottom of the cup and insert the ice-cream stick. Cut a paper heart and write a guest's name on it. Glue it on the cup.

Holiday Wrap-ups

Make your gift giving special by creating your own packaging.

TWO EASY BOWS
(ribbon, cardboard, wire)

1. Wrap ribbon around a 2-by-6-inch piece of cardboard. Cut notches at the center of both sides of the ribbon. Remove the cardboard. Twist wire around the notches. Spread out the ribbon, forming a bow.

2. Cut 8-inch strips of ribbon. Glue the ends of the strips together, making loops. Press and glue each loop in the center. Layer the loops on top of each other, and glue. Glue a small circle of ribbon in the center.

HOLIDAY STENCIL PAPER
(old newspaper, poster paper, poster board, cellulose sponge, watercolors)

1. Cover your work surface with old newspaper. Cut a large piece of poster paper and tape the corners down so the paper is flat on the newspaper.

2. To make stencils, draw and cut out holiday designs from 6-inch-square pieces of poster board, as shown. Hold a stencil on the poster paper. Dip a small piece of cellulose sponge in watercolor and dab the inside of the stencil.

3. Let the designs dry. Use the paper to wrap holiday gifts.

POTATO-PRINT SACK
(paper bag, potato, table knife, paint, ribbon)

1. Before you decorate your sack, be sure your gift will fit inside.

2. Wash and dry a potato half. Draw a simple design on a piece of paper and cut it out. Place the design on the cut side of the potato. Using a table knife, cut away the area around the design, leaving the design about a 1/2 inch above the rest of the potato.

3. Paint the potato design and press it onto the paper bag. Repeat the painting and printing. Let the paint dry before you put the gift inside.

4. Fold over the top of the sack, and punch two holes through the flap. Thread a ribbon through and tie it into a bow.

RUDOLPH GIFT BOX
(cardboard box with lid, paper, four cellophane-covered candy canes, ribbon)

1. Cover the top and sides of a box lid with paper.

2. Cut out a head for Rudolph from paper. Glue on cut-paper features. Arrange the cut-paper head and the cellophane-covered candy canes on the lid. Glue in place. Add a ribbon bow to the top of his head.

3. Cut and glue a small paper caption balloon. On it, write the word "To:" and the name of the person receiving the gift.

CUT-PAPER SURPRISE BAG
(paper bag, paper, self-adhesive reinforcement rings, yarn)

1. Before you decorate your bag, be sure your gift will fit inside.

2. Create a colorful scene by drawing and cutting out pieces of paper and gluing them to the front of the bag. Near the top, place two self-adhesive reinforcement rings. Use a paper punch and punch out the holes in the rings.

3. Close the top of the bag. Punch through the front holes to the back of the bag. Add two self-adhesive rings to the back holes. Thread a piece of yarn through the holes to make a handle.

ORNAMENT-TAGS
(plastic-foam tray, poster board, moveable plastic eyes, paper, ribbon, cookie cutter, felt, buttons, rickrack)

1. To make the Santa, cut a circle from a plastic-foam tray. Add a hat from poster board. Add moveable plastic eyes and a paper mouth and nose. Cut pieces of ribbon, curl around a pencil, and glue in place to make a beard.

2. With a paper punch, punch a hole at the top of the hat and tie a loop of ribbon.

3. To make the "gingerbread" character, place a gingerbread cookie cutter on a piece of brown poster board and trace around it. Draw another line about 1/4 inch from the traced outline and cut out the character.

4. Place the gingerbread cookie cutter on a piece of felt and trace around it. Cut out the design. Glue the felt piece on top of the poster board.

5. Add button eyes, a mouth, and buttons down his body. Add rickrack for trim. Punch a hole at the top and add a loop of rickrack. Add a sign from poster board with the recipient's name on it.

(Use these gift tags as ornaments after the presents are opened.)

MATERIAL INDEX